So Wild a Dream

Christopher Florentz

A PACEMAKER BESTELLERS™ BOOK

FEARON·PITMAN PUBLISHERS, INC.
Belmont, California

Series Director: Tom Belina
Designer: Richard Kharibian
Cover and illustrations: Cliff Spohn

ISBN–0–8224–5272–8

Library of Congress Catalog Card Number: 77-77158

Printed in the United States of America.

1. 9 8 7 6 5 4 3 2 1

CONTENTS

CHAPTER 1
THE SECRET LETTER

The dirt road that ran from Trenton to Southbridge was packed deep with snow. And still more snow was falling. In the summer the 12 mile trip from Trenton to Southbridge by wagon was fun. But it was winter now, and the trip was long and hard.

Beth Ferguson couldn't help worrying as the two old farm horses slowly pulled the wagon. Her father had been fighting in the war for almost two years. Ever since it started, in 1775. He was in General Washington's army. It seemed to Beth like the war with England would never end. She looked into the forest on both sides of the road, watching for the British. Beth felt cold all over—and not just because it was winter. She had made the trip a hundred times before. But this trip was different from all the rest.

Beth called out "giddyap" to her team of horses. Then she thought back to how it had all started two nights ago . . .

"Beth," her father had said. "A secret letter must be taken to Southbridge. General Washington needs someone who knows the road. Someone the British would never think to question . . ." It seemed to Beth like hours passed before her father spoke again. "Will you do it, Beth? If you will, General Washington wants to see you tomorrow."

"Tomorrow?" Beth answered, almost not able to believe what was happening. Sometimes it seemed like nothing ever changed on the farm. But now this! This would change everything! And it was so sudden.

Her father sat down and began to clean his gun. Then he spoke once more in a low voice. "Beth . . . You know what could happen if the British catch you?"

Beth thought for a minute. She would be carrying a secret letter from General Washington. Beth's face turned white and her heart missed a beat. She would be a spy!

Placing his hand on Beth's arm, her father spoke in a soft voice. "If the British catch you with the letter, they could hang you. If you don't want to do it, General Washington will understand." He waited for an answer.

But Beth Ferguson said nothing. She was thinking about poor Johnny Cramer from Haystown. He was 17, the same age as Beth, when the British hanged him as a spy last month.

Jacob Ferguson put down his gun. "I didn't want to ask you," he said. "But there is no one else we can count on. And that letter must get to Southbridge."

Then he walked over to the fire and threw on another log. "Think on it some tonight," he said. "I've got to be back in camp in the morning. I must know by then." Still Beth did not answer. She was thinking. Finally her eyes met those of her father.

"I'll do it," she said.

Beth didn't sleep much that night. She thought about the war. And about her father. And about Johnny Cramer. Then she began to think about all the men and women who were fighting and risking their lives for their country. And she thought about liberty. Liberty! That one word seemed to stick in Beth's mind. She wasn't sure of just what it meant. But she knew it had to do with people being free to think and act as they pleased. She knew it was so important that men and women were willing to die for it! And now she might also die for it. It was hours before she was finally able to get to sleep.

In the morning Beth and her father got up before the sun. Her mother was already fixing breakfast in the kitchen.

"What about the chickens, Pa?" she asked.

Her father smiled. "Your mother can feed the chickens today. You and I have important work to do," he said.

Beth and her father ate breakfast without talking much. Then they got the horses ready and rode out together for General Washington's camp. The snow was just starting to come down. In the early morning light it was hard to see much of anything.

Suddenly, something jumped right out in front of their horses! It was just a small animal, but it frightened the horses. Beth's father's horse jumped high in the air. His gun went flying from his hands. It hit the ground and went off with a loud bang. He cried out and fell from his horse.

"Pa!" Beth cried out. She jumped down from her horse and ran over to where her father lay

in the snow. A dark red circle covered the snow under his leg. Beth took one look at the blood and ran back to her horse. Taking a piece of rope from her saddle she returned to her father.

"Just above the wound," he said. "Tie the rope just above where you see the blood." But Beth was already fast at work. When she finished tying up the wound she helped her father back up on his horse. Beth could see that he was weak from the gun shot.

"We better get you home, Pa," she said.

But Beth's father shook his head.

"I'll be all right, Beth. It's not far back to the farm. Your mother will know what to do. But you have a meeting with General Washington!"

Beth's face began to turn red. "By myself, Pa? I've got to go and meet General Washington by myself?"

"He's a good man, Beth. A man you can trust same as you would your Pa. Now you get started for the camp. Tell General Washington what happened this morning. Tell him I'll be back as soon as I can."

Beth turned her horse back on to the road. She waved to her father. Then, starting out again for General Washington's camp, she called out, "Giddyap!"

CHAPTER **2**

The Road to Southbridge

Beth kept her horse Ginger at a fast walk. Snow was falling and the air was very cold. Her hair was pushed up under her hat. Her coat was pulled up around her face against the wind. Right now even her best friend wouldn't have known her. The sun had come up. But with the snow falling, it was still hard to see.

Suddenly, as she rode around a bend in the road, a man jumped out. He was wearing a torn old blue coat. And he was holding a gun.

"Stop!" he shouted at her.

"Giddyap," Beth shouted into Ginger's ear. "Come on, girl, giddyap!" She could see the gun in the man's hands. It was pointed right at her head. She rode right past the man, ducking down low in the saddle. Behind her there was a sharp crack. The shot buzzed by her head like an angry bee. Up the road two more men jumped out from the forest. Their guns were pointed right at her. There was nothing she could do. She would have to let them rob her. Beth stopped her horse in the road. Slowly she brought her hands up over her head.

"Get down from that horse," a voice barked from behind. It was the first man, the one who had shot at her. "Now take off your hat so we can see your face." Beth did as the man ordered.

"Well, I'll be," the man said when he saw her hair. By now the other two men had come from up the road. "Hey, Ben! Aaron! Look here," the man said. "It's a girl."

Beth felt herself shake when she saw the hole in her hat. The gun shot had come very close.

"Who are you?" one of the men said to Beth. "And what business brings you out this way?"

Beth didn't answer. Should she tell them? What if they were British?

Then the first man spoke again. "If she won't talk to us . . ." He looked at his two friends while he spoke. "Then she is going to have to do her explaining to General Washington."

Beth looked up in surprise. "General Washington?" she said. "That's who I'm on my way to see." She could feel her heart beating again.

"Would you take me to see the General, please? I'm Beth Ferguson. He knows I'm coming."

The first man shook his head with a laugh. "Well, I'll be! Boys, you stay here and watch the road. I'll take her to the General."

Before she knew it, Beth was standing in General Washington's office. It was in a small farm house. General Washington was tall. His eyes were deep and blue.

At first Beth didn't know what to say. But General Washington did most of the talking. He said he was sorry to hear about Beth's father. He was also sorry about Beth's close call. After a short time, Beth knew that her father had been right about the General. She knew she could trust him.

"Your father explained to you about the letter? It must be taken to Southbridge," General Washington said.

"Yes," Beth answered. "I understand."

"And you know what could happen to you if you're caught?"

"Yes," she answered again.

"And it's not just the British you will have to watch out for," General Washington said. "There are many people living in Southbridge who side with the British. People who would do anything in their power to stop us from winning the war. They would be happy to turn you over to the British."

Beth said nothing. General Washington could see that she had made up her mind and would not change it.

The General came over and stood in front of Beth. "Your father told me that you make trips to Southbridge all the time for supplies."

"That's right," Beth said. "People see me on that road all the time."

"That's why I'm sending you with the letter. No one will think that it's strange if you go to pick up supplies. But don't talk to too many people. And be careful of what you say."

General Washington went over to his desk and picked up a small white letter. Handing it to Beth, he spoke slowly, almost in a whisper. "Take this letter to Gregory Hanlon. He is the silversmith in Southbridge. Wait while he gives you an answer to bring me."

After she had taken the letter, General Washington said, "The fight for liberty is in your hands. Good luck, and God be with you!"

The ride home didn't seem as long. It had stopped snowing, and Beth was happy. "The

fight for liberty is in your hands," the General had said.

She looked up at the cold gray sky. She could tell that there was more snow yet to come. It would make the trip to Southbridge tomorrow long and hard.

When Beth got back to the farm her father was resting. Her mother had cleaned and taken care of his wound. He was going to be all right. They wanted to know everything that General Washington had said to her. Both her mother and her father were afraid that the British would catch her. Beth could see it in their eyes. But she could see something else in their eyes, too. She could see they were pleased she had decided to take part in the fight for liberty.

Now Beth was on her way to Southbridge. "Only a few more hours," she said to herself. She looked around for British soldiers again. The secret letter was in a special pocket. Her mother had sewn the pocket into her coat. Even if she were stopped by the British, they would never find the letter. Or so she hoped.

The British army was camped by the Assunpink River, not far from Southbridge. General Cornwallis was the head of the British army. General Cornwallis was trying to get his army back into fighting shape. They had just lost the Battle of Trenton against General Washington's army.

They lost in part because of the work of American spies. General Cornwallis wasn't planning on losing any more battles. Or letting any more spies get to General Washington.

All this Beth knew. She thought about Johnny Cramer. He had been caught spying by the British. And they had hanged him.

Beth became afraid. Her blood ran cold. She thought she heard the sound of horses from far off. She stopped the wagon and listened.

But it was only the wind and the blowing snow. She kept on looking for British soldiers, but she saw no one.

It was afternoon when she reached Southbridge. Her first stop would be Pierce's Store. There she would buy farm supplies. That was why she had come to Southbridge. At least that was the story she would use to cover up the real reason.

Beth hoped Mr. Pierce wouldn't be in the store today. He was a strange man. He had been a friend of her father before the war. But the two men didn't see things the same way any more. That was all right with Beth. She had never liked Mr. Pierce anyway. She hoped that his son Willie would be in the store instead. Willie was not too smart. But he was kind of nice in his own way.

Beth brought the wagon to a stop in front of Pierce's Store. She tied the horses to the post in front. Stamping the snow from her boots, she went inside. It felt good and warm after her trip. At first the store seemed empty. Beth looked around the place. She felt cold all over when Mr. Pierce came walking slowly out from the back room.

CHAPTER 3
THE SILVERSMITH SPY

"Well, now, if it isn't Beth Ferguson," John Pierce said. "What brings you all the way to Southbridge on a day like this? The roads must be pretty bad with all this snow."

Right off Beth felt like she was in trouble. It was the way Mr. Pierce made his voice sound.

"We need some supplies for the farm, Mr. Pierce," Beth answered. "Pa thought the snow would hold. I left before it started."

John Pierce looked closely at Beth. "How is your Pa?" he said. "It's been almost a year since I saw him last. Funny he never comes to town anymore."

Beth knew she had to think fast. "Well, he was sick for a long time. Then the axle on the wagon broke. And the roof needed fixing." She wanted to say just enough to Mr. Pierce. But not too much.

"The axle on the wagon broke?" Mr. Pierce asked. He seemed interested.

"Yes," Beth said. "It was a big job for Pa, what with being sick and all."

"I guess it would be," Mr. Pierce said. "Tell me, anything much happening down Trenton way? Your Pa have any idea what George Washington is up to? He sure is a funny one, old George." Then Mr. Pierce gave a mean laugh. "Those farmers that George calls his army sure are a sad lot!"

Beth could feel her face getting red. But she couldn't let him know how she really felt. "Can't say as how I know much about that, Mr. Pierce. Things have been pretty busy on the farm. We haven't had much time to keep up with the war." Beth felt she had herself under control now. "I just hope they all stay clear of our farm. Long as they leave us alone!" Beth knew that was the kind of talk Mr. Pierce wanted to hear.

John Pierce gave a short laugh. "You just wait till General Cornwallis gets hold of those farmers. His army is a *real* army, not a bunch of farmers. Next time the British army will cut those farmers to pieces."

Beth wanted to ask John Pierce if he had forgotten about the Battle of Trenton, which Washington's army had just won. But she knew it was best to say nothing.

She waited a few seconds and then said, "Now about the supplies . . ."

Mr. Pierce got out all the supplies that Beth needed. Then he helped her put them into the wagon outside.

"It's a long trip back to your farm. Why don't you have a cup of tea before you go? I'll just heat up some water and–"

"Oh, no thank you," Beth said right away. "That's very kind of you. But I want to stop off and say hello to my friend Elizabeth Sims. Then I better be getting home."

"All right, Beth," John Pierce said with a cold smile. "You do that. You go and have a nice visit with your friend Elizabeth. Guess you don't get to see much of each other. And have a safe trip home."

Beth left the wagon in front of the store. It wasn't far to Gregory Hanlon's silversmith shop. But she didn't walk right to the shop. Instead she walked toward Elizabeth Sims' house. Then she made her way around to the back of the silversmith's shop. This way Mr. Pierce wouldn't see where she was going.

When she got to the shop, Beth stopped outside. The window was filled with beautiful silver dishes and cups. Gregory Hanlon, the silversmith, had made these cups and dishes with his hands. Beth looked around to make sure no one was watching her. Then she went inside. A young man sat at a table, working. Beth looked around the shop until the man got up from his work. He was tall, with strong, firm hands. His eyes were deep brown, like his hair.

"Good afternoon," he said, coming over to Beth. "What can I do for you?"

"Mr. Hanlon?" Beth asked slowly.

"Yes," the silversmith said with a warm smile. "May I help you?"

Beth looked around again, to make sure they were alone in the shop. Then she looked at the silversmith and said in a low voice, "On land or on sea we shall fight to be free."

The secret words took Gregory Hanlon by surprise. He stepped back for a minute. Could this girl really be a spy? he wondered.

There was a look in Beth's eyes that gave him his answer.

"What be the cause?" he asked. This was the second part of the secret greeting.

"The dream of liberty." Beth said.

Gregory Hanlon gave Beth's hand a warm shake. "Come with me, please," he said. He walked to the back of the shop. He opened a door which led into another room. It was the part of the building where the silversmith lived. Beth followed him into the room. He closed the door behind them.

"My name is Beth Ferguson, Mr. Hanlon," she said. "General Washington sent me." Beth took out the secret letter and handed it to him.

The silversmith pointed to a chair in the corner. "Why don't you sit down? I know you've had a long trip."

Then, as he opened the secret letter, he said, "Would you like a cup of tea? The tea pot is on the fire and the water is hot."

"Yes, thanks, Mr. Hanlon," Beth answered.

"Call me Gregory. And I'll call you Beth. After all, we are both spies," he said with a warm laugh.

Beth liked the silversmith right from the start. But she didn't much care to be called a spy. Even if it was true.

Gregory Hanlon sat back in a large easy chair to read the letter. "So, it's to be Princeton next," he said in a low voice. He read the rest of the letter without speaking again. Then he made tea for the two of them. He gave Beth her tea. They sat and talked for a while. Then Gregory went over to his desk. He sat down and took out a piece of paper. He wrote his answer to General Washington.

When he finished, he came back over to Beth. "General Washington must get this letter by

tomorrow morning, Beth. If anything happens and he doesn't get the letter . . . I'm afraid many of our men will die if that should happen."

Beth took the letter. "General Washington will have this letter by morning," she said.

"Good luck, then," the silversmith said. "I hope we see each other again soon. God be with you, Beth."

"Good-bye, Gregory." She gave him a warm smile. She hoped she would see him again soon, too. Very soon.

As she left the shop, Beth again looked around to see if anyone was watching. The sky was starting to grow dark. And it looked like there might be more snow.

Beth had wanted to see her friend Elizabeth Sims before she left. But now she wondered if she should. Could she keep from telling her best friend that she had become a spy? Beth wasn't sure. And she had Gregory Hanlon's secret letter with her. What if . . . ? No, Beth decided. She had better not push her luck. Many men might die if she didn't get the letter to General Washington. Her own father might be one of them! Beth turned away from Elizabeth Sims' house and walked toward the wagon.

CHAPTER 4
THE TRIP HOME

The snow looked like it was going to hold up for a while. Beth felt better about spying after meeting Gregory Hanlon. He had seemed so sure of himself and of the cause. So Gregory Hanlon was the Southbridge spy. She would never have guessed it. The British had been trying to find out who the Southbridge spy was for a year. Now Beth knew the secret. And because she did, Gregory Hanlon's very life was in her hands. Beth felt a special feeling for the young silversmith. It was a strange, beautiful feeling that she had never felt before.

As she walked toward her wagon, Beth saw two men near it. She could make out one of them. It was Mr. Pierce! The other one was looking up under her wagon. She couldn't see who it was. Then Mr. Pierce saw her. He said something to the man under the wagon. When the other man stood up, Beth could see that it was Willie Pierce.

"They must be looking at the axle," she said to herself. She knew they would see that the axle had not been broken. Mr. Pierce would know that she had lied.

Just before Beth reached them, Mr. Pierce said to Willie, "Son, I want you to do two things real quick. First, go over to the Sims' house. Ask Elizabeth if her friend Beth Ferguson has been by for a visit. Then you run over to Mr. Sweet's place. Tell him everything I told you. He will know what to do."

"But, Pa!" Willie said.

"You just do as I say!" Mr. Pierce said in a mean voice.

"Yes, Pa."

Beth saw Willie turn and leave. Mr. Pierce must have told him to do something for him. Beth knew that Willie was afraid of his father. But something was up. Willie would never run off without first saying hello to Beth.

Mr. Pierce gave her that strange smile of his. "Why, hello again. Did you have a nice visit with Elizabeth?"

Beth knew she had to keep herself under control. “As a matter of fact, no,” she said. “Elizabeth wasn’t home. I talked with her mother instead.”

“Is that right? Not home?” Mr. Pierce said. “Too bad.”

Then he pointed at the wagon. “Willie and I were just taking a look at your wagon. Your Pa did a real fine job on the axle. Why, it almost looks like it was never even broken,” he said with a laugh. “A real fine job!”

Mr. Pierce waited for Beth to answer. But she just climbed up into the wagon.

“Don’t go yet,” John Pierce said. “Come inside for a minute. I want to show you something. Got a new plow. Just came in from Philadelphia last week.”

Beth looked up at the sky. “It’s getting late, Mr. Pierce,” she said. “I really should be getting home. My mother and father will worry about me if I stay too long.”

Mr. Pierce stepped inside the front door of his store. “It will only take a minute,” he said. “I want you to tell your father about it.” Now Mr. Pierce was acting like an old friend. The way he did before the war had started. Beth didn't know what to do.

"Mark my words. This new plow will make your work real easy this spring. I know your Pa will want to hear about it."

Beth got down from the wagon. She would only stay a few minutes. Maybe Mr. Pierce would forget about the axle.

Beth went back into the store with Mr. Pierce. He told Beth all about the new plow. It took him a half hour to explain everything. Then when Beth tried to leave the store, he stopped her at the door.

"Oh, I almost forgot. I have some pretty cloth for your mother. She ordered it some time ago. It just came in. It will make a beautiful dress. I'll cut it for her. Just be a minute, Beth."

As she turned away from the door, a man on a horse rode past the store. It looked like Mr. Sweet's horse, Lightning. But the man riding it looked like Willie Pierce. Why would Willie be riding Mr. Sweet's horse? Maybe it wasn't Willie. It was getting dark and she couldn't really be sure . . .

Another half hour passed before Beth left for home. Willie had never returned to the store.

But Mr. Pierce had been very nice to her. Beth didn't know what to think.

The trip home wouldn't take as long. The two horses knew they were going back to the farm. Then they would eat and go to sleep. They both pulled the wagon down the road at a fast walk.

"Giddyap, Ginger, Giddyap, Dusty," she called to the horses. The letter from Gregory Hanlon was in her secret pocket. Mr. Pierce wasn't going to stop her from getting that letter to General Washington.

She smiled to herself. Not even the whole British army would stop her!

CHAPTER 5
CAUGHT

Willie Pierce never dreamed a horse could be so fast. It was only the second time Mr. Sweet had ever let him ride Lightning. The road that led to the Assunpink River flew by. Soon he would be in the camp of General Cornwallis.

Everything had happened so fast. Willie didn't even have time to think about what he was doing. First he had gone over to the Sims house. Elizabeth said she hadn't seen Beth in a long time. Then he ran over to Mr. Sweet's place. Willie told Mr. Sweet everything his father had told him to say.

"By the power of King George, we have got him!" Mr. Sweet had shouted.

"Who have we got?" Willie asked.

"The Southbridge spy, son, that's who! That little farm girl must know the name of the Southbridge spy. She is going to give us his name, or else. General Cornwallis will see to that! Yes, sir, we have got him now."

As Willie rode toward the Assunpink he was afraid for Beth. He liked her very much. She was the only girl Willie could really talk to. And it was the look in Mr. Sweet's eyes that worried him most. He was afraid the British would hurt her. He didn't want that.

Willie tried to make himself feel better. "They won't hurt Beth," he said to himself. "General Cornwallis will just talk to her. They just want to know who the Southbridge spy is."

Then Willie remembered how the British had hanged Johnny Cramer. Willie had felt bad about it for a long time. He wouldn't talk to anyone and he wouldn't eat. He could only think about the fun he and Johnny used to have together. But his Pa and Mr. Sweet both said that Johnny had it coming. He had been a spy and that was that.

"Why did they have to hang him?" Willie said. "They could have just put him in jail."

Suddenly Willie brought Lightning to a stop. The moon was starting to come up over the tops of the trees. "What if they hang Beth like they did Johnny?" Willie said. He gave Lightning's head a pat. "We could just take our time, Lightning," he said to the horse. "That would give Beth enough time to get back to the farm."

But then Willie thought about his Pa. He knew his Pa would give him a real bad beating. Willie had gotten bad beatings before. Once his Pa beat him so bad he couldn't walk for three days. Willie wanted to help Beth with all his heart. But he was more afraid of his Pa than anything else in the world. Tears came to Willie's eyes. He shook his head slowly.

"I'm sorry, Beth," he whispered. Willie wiped away his tears. "Giddyap, Lightning. Giddyap, boy." Willie started out for the Assunpink River. Once again the road flew by in the cold winter night.

It wasn't long before Willie reached the British camp. He told a British soldier that he was from Southbridge. He said that he was carrying an important letter for General Cornwallis. The soldier took him to General Cornwallis right away.

The General's eyes grew hard as he read the letter which Mr. Sweet had written. He finished the letter and looked up at Willie. "Do you know this young woman, Beth Ferguson?" he asked Willie.

"Yes, sir, General Cornwallis," Willie answered, almost in a whisper.

The General tapped on his desk with his hand. "Do you think she can tell us who the Southbridge spy is?"

Willie didn't answer General Cornwallis. He felt afraid again for Beth. His eyes couldn't look at the General. Instead he looked down at the floor. He didn't know what to say.

General Cornwallis seemed to understand Willie's feelings. "Son, no one will hurt your friend," he said. "But I must talk with her. It is men like the Southbridge spy who keep us from winning the war. Many British soldiers have been killed because of the work this spy has done. He must be stopped."

Still Willie said nothing. General Cornwallis looked at him closely. "Willie," the General said. "If your friend can tell us his name, that won't make her a spy. Do you understand?"

"I guess so," Willie said slowly.

"Good," General Cornwallis said. "Then where is she now?"

"On the road to Trenton," Willie answered. "But you won't hurt her, will you?"

"No," General Cornwallis said. "I just want to talk to her. Then she will be free to go home."

General Cornwallis called to one of his soldiers just outside the door. "Captain Anderson," the General said.

"Yes, sir," the soldier answered, stepping into the room.

"Take five men. There is a young woman driving along the Trenton road in a wagon. Her name is Beth Ferguson. Bring her back to me as fast as you can."

"Yes, sir," Captain Anderson answered. "Right away, sir!"

The soldier left the General's office.

General Cornwallis turned back to Willie. "You've done a good job, son. Many lives will be saved because of what you told me. You are a fine young man."

General Cornwallis shook Willie's hand. "Why don't you sit by the fire outside with my men and rest a while?" the General said. "If you like, stay for the night."

"Yes, sir. And thank you, sir."

Willie was happier than he had been in a long time. Wait until he told his father what General Cornwallis had said to him. Willie went out by the fire. He sat next to some of the British soldiers and talked. He began to feel like he was one of them. Before long, Willie forgot about his friend Beth.

Beth was cold and tired. And she knew her family would be worried. But it would be two more hours before she was home. "Giddyap, Ginger, Dusty," she called to the horses.

She came to the road that ran down from the Assunpink River. Beth knew the British army was up there. She made sure not to make a wrong turn. The last place she wanted to end up was in the British camp.

The moon was a bright, cold blue color. Beth could see almost as well as if it were during the day. There wasn't going to be any snow tonight after all. That was for sure. She would take the letter from Gregory Hanlon to General Washington first thing in the morning.

From back up the road Beth thought she heard the sound of horses. "It's just the wind again," she said to herself. But when she looked up, the wind wasn't blowing in the trees. She stopped the wagon and listened. The sound was still far off. It got louder as she listened. She knew it was the sound of horses on the run. There were several, maybe four or five.

Beth's heart began to pound. "Giddyap, Ginger, Dusty!" she said. "Come on, giddyap, you two! Giddyap!"

The two horses jumped into a run. Beth kept calling to the horses. Every so often she would look back up the road. All she saw was snow, trees, and a winter moon. Just a little more, she thought. If it's the British, they won't follow me too close to Trenton.

"Come on, Dusty, run!" Beth shouted. Finally she could see Sutter's Pond. Once she reached the pond, she knew she would be safe. She took one more look back up the road. Suddenly her heart jumped! Six men on horses were right behind her.

"Oh dear God," Beth cried, "Dear God! British soldiers!"

Beth was going as fast as she could. But the soldiers were catching up.

Now Beth had reached Sutter's Pond. But the British soldiers kept on coming after her!

She knew that this was it. The first soldier caught up to her wagon. He raised his gun. Then he called out to Beth, "Stop or I'll shoot!"

Beth pulled the wagon over to the side of the road. The rest of the British soldiers rode up.

"Step down from the wagon, please," the first soldier said. It was Captain Anderson.

When she got down, Captain Anderson pointed to the wagon. "Men, search the wagon," he said. Then, to Beth he said, "Are you Beth Ferguson?"

"Yes," Beth answered.

"You will have to come with us," Captain Anderson said.

"Why?" Beth asked. "What have I done? I'm just bringing supplies back to our farm."

"General Cornwallis wants to see you," Captain Anderson said. "We have orders to bring you back to camp."

Before she knew what was happening, one of the British soldiers got up into her wagon. "You will ride that horse," Captain Anderson said. He pointed to the horse the soldier in her wagon had been on. "I must tell you, do not try to escape. We have our orders to bring you back to General Cornwallis. If you try to escape, we will have to shoot you!"

Beth tried to look cool and in control. But her heart was pounding and her hands were shaking. "Why should I try to escape?" she said. "I have done nothing."

Beth got up on the British soldier's horse. The other men rode on both sides of her, their guns at the ready. Nothing more was said. They turned their horses back down the road toward the British camp.

As they rode along, Beth started to think about Johnny Cramer. Then she began to think about Gregory Hanlon. She knew she would have to be brave for Gregory. If they found out he was the Southbridge spy, they would hang him. Her mind was all mixed up. But she started to feel less afraid. Thinking about Gregory made her feel brave.

They were just about back to the British camp now. Beth had a funny feeling all over. It was like a big, warm smile that filled her up inside. She knew that she should be afraid. But somehow she wasn't. Suddenly it hit Beth. She knew it was time to ask herself an important question: Was she in love with Gregory Hanlon?

CHAPTER 6
A Last Chance

The fires in the British camp burned strong and hot. Groups of soldiers sat close around each fire, trying to keep warm. The winter night was very cold. Beth was taken to the small house that General Cornwallis used as his office. She looked at the men sitting around the fires. Her eyes came upon a face she knew. Beth had to look twice. She couldn't believe it. But there sitting at one of the fires was Willie Pierce!

Her own friend had turned her over to the British. At first Beth was so angry she felt like crying. Willie saw her and got up from the fire. He started to come toward her. Fighting back the tears, she felt herself become more and more angry.

"Don't worry, Beth," Willie started to say. "Nothing is going to happen to you . . ."

But Beth's face was red hot like the fire. She looked at Willie with hard eyes. "I thought you were my friend!" she said in a sharp voice. Then she turned to Captain Anderson. "Let's not keep General Cornwallis waiting."

Willie just stood there. "Don't worry, Beth. He just wants to talk to you, that's all . . ."

General Cornwallis was not like Beth thought he would be. In fact she thought he was very much like General Washington. He spoke in a low voice with great control. He sat at his desk which was covered with maps and paper. On one end of the desk was an oil lamp.

"Beth Ferguson?" the General said.

"Yes," Beth answered.

The General smiled at her. "Miss Ferguson, I'd just like to ask you a few questions," he said. "Then you will be free to go home. You have nothing to be afraid of." The General looked down at the papers on his desk. "Now first of all, what were you doing in Southbridge?"

"I had to pick up supplies for our farm, sir," Beth answered.

"With all this snow?" General Cornwallis asked. "Did your family think it would be safe on a day like this?"

Beth knew she had to answer the questions with great care. She couldn't let herself be tricked into saying the wrong thing. "We were all out of supplies, sir," she answered. "My father thought the snow was going to hold up. So did I. I always take the wagon to Southbridge for supplies."

"I see," General Cornwallis said. "Did you know about the spy in Southbridge?" he asked her, letting the words come slowly.

"A spy? In Southbridge? Why, no sir," Beth answered. "I know of no spy."

She was putting on a good act. General Cornwallis came from around his desk. "Miss Ferguson," he said in a firm voice. "I am talking about the spy in Southbridge who works for General Washington. He is called the Southbridge Spy. Do you know his name?"

Beth could see that the General was getting angry. She began to worry. "No, sir. I know of no spy in Southbridge," she said.

The General's voice became louder. "Is it that you do not know his name, Miss Ferguson? Or is it that you will not tell!" General Cornwallis didn't wait for Beth to answer him. "Captain Anderson," he called.

The soldier came back into the room. "What did you find in Miss Ferguson's wagon?" General Cornwallis asked the Captain.

"Farm supplies, sir," Captain Anderson answered. "There were only farm supplies in the wagon. Nothing more."

General Cornwallis tapped his foot on the floor. Beth didn't know how long she could keep up her act. "Take off your coat, please," the General said to her.

Beth followed the order.

"Captain Anderson," General Cornwallis said. "Take Miss Ferguson's coat and search it."

Beth felt sick inside as the soldier began to search her coat. She hoped against hope that he would not find the letter.

Captain Anderson searched the coat for several minutes but found nothing. He was about to put the coat down. "Just a minute," he said suddenly. "I think I've got something. Feels like a secret pocket inside."

Beth's heart missed a beat. She knew if he found the pocket he would find the letter next. Beth's hands began to shake when Captain Anderson pulled out the letter from Gregory Hanlon. He gave it to General Cornwallis. The

General opened the letter and read it. There was a funny look on his face. Beth could see that General Cornwallis didn't understand the letter. Gregory Hanlon had used a secret code.

"What does this letter mean, Miss Ferguson?" General Cornwallis asked.

"I don't know, sir," Beth answered.

General Cornwallis shook the letter at Beth. "Who gave this to you?" General Cornwallis asked.

Beth looked around the room trying to think of something to say.

"I ask you again, Miss Ferguson. Who gave you this letter?"

Beth was trapped, and she knew it. "I don't remember, sir," Beth answered.

For a minute, General Cornwallis looked mad enough to have Beth shot! After a few minutes the General got himself under control. He sat down at his desk again. He did not speak for a while. Then he began to question Beth again. He asked her questions for another hour. Beth was tired. She wanted to sleep.

Finally, the General got up from his desk. He walked over to Beth and stood in front of her. "Do you understand what it means to be caught as a spy?" he asked her.

"Yes," Beth said slowly.

"I could forget that you ever had this letter . . . But you must tell me who the Southbridge Spy is."

Beth was more frightened than she had ever been in her life. But if she told the General who had given her the letter, they would hang Gregory. It was as simple as that. "Sir," she said. "I do not remember who gave me the letter. I do not know who the Southbridge Spy is." General Cornwallis placed his hand on Beth's arm. "Beth," he said in a soft voice. "Is there anything more important to you than your own life?"

Beth looked up into the General's eyes. She knew he was giving her a last chance. She was frightened, but she answered in a firm voice.

"Yes, there is, sir," she said. "Liberty."

For several minutes General Cornwallis could not talk. The great British general had never before known a young woman as brave as Beth. "I see . . ." he finally said. "I'm sorry, Miss Ferguson."

Then he began to walk from one side of the room to the other. "Captain Anderson," he called. When the soldier came into the room, General Cornwallis looked at him with sad eyes. "Captain," he said. "You must be present while I sentence Miss Ferguson."

"Yes, sir," Captain Anderson answered.

"Miss Ferguson," the General said, walking around his desk. "Your trip to Southbridge was most strange. You lied twice to Mr. Pierce. You spent time in Southbridge with a person you will not name. A secret letter was found in your coat. You will not even tell me what the letter means. But most important of all, you will not tell me the person who gave you the letter."

The British General stopped in the center of the small room. He ran his hand in his hair. "Miss Ferguson, I have given you more than enough chance to save yourself. I find you guilty of being a spy for the Continental Army under General Washington. I order you to be hanged by the neck until dead. The sentence will be carried out tomorrow morning at first light."

CHAPTER 7
THE REVEREND MORLEY

Word was quick to spread around the British camp. A spy would be hanged in the morning. And the spy was a young woman!

Willie Pierce couldn't believe his ears. General Cornwallis had said nothing would happen to Beth. And now she was to be hanged!

Willie made his way around the fires that still burned. Many of the soldiers had gone to sleep. When he got to General Cornwallis' office, a soldier stopped him.

"What's on your mind, son?" the soldier asked him.

"I must see General Cornwallis. It's very important," Willie answered.

The soldier just smiled at him. "I'm afraid that's not possible. The General has gone to sleep for the night. You will have to wait until morning to see him."

"I can't wait until morning," Willie said. "It's about the young woman who is going to be hanged. In the morning will be too late!"

The soldier just shook his head. "First off, the General has already decided to hang that spy," the soldier said. "Nothing is going to change that. And second, no one wakes up General Cornwallis once he goes to sleep. That's what I'm here for." The soldier gave his gun a pat. "Now you just go on off and get some sleep," he said. "Go on, now!"

Willie knew he had to do something fast. They were going to hang Beth because of him. He ran to where Lightning was tied up. He told the soldier on watch that he had to get back home. Willie started out for Southbridge on the run. If only there is enough time, he thought.

"Come on, Lightning, move! Giddyap, boy, giddyap!" he shouted to the horse. The miles flew by. Willie could think of only one thing. He knew there was only one man who could save Beth now—the Southbridge Spy! But Willie didn't even know who the spy was. And morning was only a few hours away.

When he reached Southbridge, Willie went to the Sims' house. The house was dark. Everyone was sleeping. Willie had to knock for a long time before Mr. Sims came to the door.

"Willie Pierce!" he said. "Now, what do you want at this time of night?"

"It's Beth Ferguson, Mr. Sims. I've just come from the British camp. They're going to hang her in the morning," he said. "They want to know the name of the Southbridge Spy. She won't tell them. So they're going to hang her."

Elizabeth, Beth's best friend, came down the stairs. When she heard the news, she shouted, "The Reverend Morley! He will know what to do, Pa. I've got to see the Reverend!"

Elizabeth pulled on her clothes and ran from the house. She didn't stop until she got to the Reverend Morley's house. She pounded on the door until a light came on.

Reverend Morley was still half asleep as he opened the door. "What is it, child?" the Reverend asked her in surprise.

Elizabeth told him what had happened. "Can we save Beth, Reverend Morley?" she asked in a frightened voice. At first the Reverend didn't answer. He sat deep in thought. Who could the Southbridge Spy be? he asked himself. The Reverend knew only one man in Southbridge who felt the way he did. He had talked in secret many times about the cause of liberty with Gregory Hanlon. That's who it must be, Reverend Morley thought. Gregory Hanlon must be the Southbridge Spy!

"You must go home now, Elizabeth," he said. "I will do what I can."

Elizabeth looked at the Reverend with hope. But he shook his head. "Go home and pray for your friend, Elizabeth. Go home. It is God's will which shall be done."

Reverend Morley put on his coat as they left the house. He made sure no one was watching him. Then he walked over to Gregory Hanlon's shop and knocked on the door.

In a few minutes he was inside, telling Gregory Hanlon the news. When the silversmith heard that Beth was going to be hanged his eyes and face burned.

"There is only one reason you came to tell me this, Reverend," Gregory said. "You must have guessed that I am the Southbridge Spy."

Reverend Morley was slow to answer.

"It does not matter now, Reverend," Gregory said. "I must try to save Beth. Please wait one minute while I get dressed."

Gregory Hanlon stepped into the back room. He dressed as fast as he could. Then he took secret maps and papers from a desk. Walking over to the fire, he threw them in. He must not leave anything important behind for the British to find.

Then he went back out into the front room. "Reverend," he said. "I must ride for the British camp right away. The sun will be up in two hours. There isn't much time."

"I understand, Gregory," the Reverend said. "You are a brave man. You have given much more than most men for the cause of liberty. May God be with you, my son!"

The moon filled the silversmith's shop with a soft, blue light. The two men shook hands, and then Gregory Hanlon left. He had to make it to the British camp by morning. Beth would be hanged if he did not.

"She could have saved herself," Gregory said to himself as he rode hard toward the British camp. "She could have given them my name."

Gregory had had a feeling about Beth the first day they met. Now he was sure. Beth Ferguson was the kind of woman he wanted to be his wife. But he knew that it would never be possible for Beth to be his wife. Not now. The British would hang him first.

"Giddyap!" he shouted to his horse. Gregory had no time to lose. His only thought was to save Beth. He must reach the camp by morning. It was cold but the sky was clear. Gregory didn't feel the cold air. He only knew how he felt about Beth. And it did not matter what might happen to him.

CHAPTER 8
LIBERTY AND LOVE

It was just before morning when Gregory Hanlon reached the British camp. The soldiers were starting to get up. Some of them were already eating breakfast. The sky was gray and light snow was coming down.

"I must see General Cornwallis," Gregory said to one of the soldiers.

The British General had been up long before first light. Gregory was led to the General's office. For several minutes he stood facing General Cornwallis. General Cornwallis was studying some papers on his desk. Finally, the General looked up and spoke.

"Yes, what is it?" he asked the silversmith. General Cornwallis thought Gregory was a member of Beth's family.

Gregory Hanlon looked the General in the eye. "You must not hang Beth Ferguson," he said.

General Cornwallis looked at Gregory in surprise. "Why must I not hang her?" the General asked. "She is a spy!"

The silversmith shook his head at the General. "She didn't know what she was doing. Beth Ferguson is not a spy. I have come to speak for her."

"Who are you?" the General asked.

"I am Gregory Hanlon. To some I am known as the Southbridge Spy."

General Cornwallis got up to look at Gregory. The General's eyes were wide with surprise. "I see," was all General Cornwallis could say. He had never known such brave men and women. First Beth Ferguson had been willing to die for the cause of liberty. Now this young man stood before him saying that he was the Southbridge Spy.

"What kind of people are you Americans, Mr. Hanlon?" General Cornwallis asked. "Does living or dying mean nothing to you?"

"What kind of people are we? We are a people who would be free, sir," Gregory answered. "We are a people who dream of liberty. And we will die for that dream, if we have to."

"A wild dream," the General said. "But a grand one, too, I must say, to fill people's hearts with such feelings."

General Cornwallis looked Gregory in the eye. "If only we could have met in another place and time, Mr. Hanlon," he said. Then he walked back to his desk. "Mr. Hanlon, I am sorry. But this is war. I am a general of the British army. You know what I must do."

Gregory felt his heart sink. "I understand, sir," he said in a low voice. "You have your side. I have mine. I am an American spy and you are a British general. Each of us has a job to do."

"I am glad you feel that way," General Cornwallis said. "You are a good and brave man. But war is war."

Gregory Hanlon moved close to the General's desk. "Sir, about Beth Ferguson," Gregory said.

"You have my word, Mr. Hanlon, as a soldier and as a man. Beth will be set free. Captain Anderson!" the General called.

The Captain came into the room. "Mr. Hanlon," the General said. "Is there anything I can do before you die?"

"Yes, sir," Gregory answered. "I would like to see Beth one more time."

"You shall have your wish. But first I must sentence you."

Then General Cornwallis spoke in a low yet firm voice. "Mr. Gregory Hanlon, I find you guilty by your own word of being the Southbridge Spy. I order you to be hanged by the neck until dead in one hour."

General Cornwallis looked over at Captain Anderson. "Bring Miss Ferguson here."

A few minutes later the soldier returned with Beth. "Gregory!" she cried.

She and Gregory walked toward each other slowly. They met in the center of the room.

"Captain Anderson," General Cornwallis said. "Let's wait outside."

Beth's eyes filled with tears. She put her arms around Gregory's neck. "You shouldn't have come," she whispered.

Gregory looked deep into her eyes. "I had to come, Beth," he answered. "I had to come because . . . *I love you.*"

"Oh, Gregory," Beth said. "I love you, too!"

Then she cried as he held her in his arms.

They kissed. Then they looked into each other's eyes without speaking. There was no need for words.

After a long time Gregory looked around the room. It was time to think about the war again. His job was not yet finished. Neither was Beth's. And they both knew it.

"Beth," Gregory whispered to her. "Did they take the letter from you?"

"Yes," she answered.

"Do you remember everything I wrote in that letter?"

"Yes, I think so," Beth answered.

"Good," Gregory said. "You must go to General Washington right away. You must tell him everything I wrote in that letter."

Beth looked up at Gregory. "You have my word," she said. "It shall be done."

The door opened and Captain Anderson looked into the room

"I'm sorry, Mr. Hanlon. But it's time . . ."

Gregory looked over at the soldier. "Yes, of course," Gregory said. Then he looked down again at Beth. "There are two things which you must always hold dear, Beth. Liberty, and love. Some say both are just wild dreams. But you and I know better."

"Yes, my love, we do," Beth said. "And neither is so wild a dream."

Beth wiped her eyes with her hand. She reached up and kissed Gregory one last time. Then she tried to smile.

"Good-bye, Beth," Gregory said in a soft voice. "You best go now."

Beth touched his arm. "Good-bye, Gregory . . . Good-bye, my love . . ."

Captain Anderson led Gregory Hanlon from the room. He was taken outside and brought to the tree in the center of camp where men were hanged. The British soldiers took their hats off when Gregory Hanlon walked past them. Even when men fight on different sides, a brave man is always honored.

General Cornwallis came back into his office where Beth still stood. "Miss Ferguson," he said. "You are free to go at any time. If you wish, you may stay with Gregory until the end. It is up to you."

Beth tried to think what Gregory would want her to do. Deep down inside she knew. He would want her to leave right away for General Washington. "I think I'll go home," Beth said.

The General took off his hat to Beth. "I understand, Miss Ferguson," he said in a soft but firm voice. "I can only say that you and Mr. Hanlon are both very brave. I hope that all your soldiers are not so brave. For if they are, England can never hope to win the war!"

They left the General's office. General Cornwallis walked with Beth to her wagon.

"A safe trip home, Miss Ferguson," the General said. "And may God be with you!"

As Beth got up into her wagon, she could hear the roll of the drums. It meant that they were ready to hang Gregory. She looked back to where the hanging tree was. Then she turned back to her horses. Beth didn't know if she was brave enough to watch them hang the man she loved. There were tears in her eyes.

"Giddyap, Ginger. Giddyap, Dusty," she called to her horses.

As she turned down the road that led to Trenton, the sound of the drums stopped. Gregory Hanlon was no more.

Beth drove for two hours before she reached the camp of General Washington. When she got there she told the General all that had happened. She wanted to cry again, but Gregory wouldn't have wanted that. The General listened to her story without speaking. Then she told him what Gregory had written in the secret letter. General Washington looked at Beth with great surprise.

"Beth, words cannot speak to you my feelings right now," the General said. Then he put his arms around Beth and kissed her head.

Turning to one of his men, General Washington said, "We leave for Princeton tonight!" Then he looked down at Beth. "Would you like to come with us?"

She thought of Gregory and shook her head yes. "More than anything in the world, General Washington," Beth said.

"Good," the General said. "Why don't you sleep for a while? You're going to need it."

"Yes, sir," Beth answered.

Late that night, General Washington gave the order. His men were to leave their fires burning all night while they marched on Princeton. The British would see the fires burning. They wouldn't think General Washington's army had even left their camp. They wouldn't be ready for the attack. Beth was given a horse and she rode with the General. By morning they reached Princeton.

General Washington pointed with his hand toward the town of Princeton. Then he said to Beth, "If we win, it will be because of Gregory Hanlon." The General called out to his men in a loud, strong voice. "Men, begin the attack!"

The whole army moved toward the town. The battle had begun and General Washington's men began to storm the British-held town. Guns roared on both sides.

Beth sat on a hill just outside of Princeton. She could see everything that happened. By late morning, General Washington's army had won the battle. The smoke from the guns cleared over the battle very slowly. And in the cold winter air, Beth could feel Gregory standing behind her. He had been watching the battle with her.

She listened hard, and she could hear his low, soft voice whispering like the wind. “There are two things which you must always hold dear,” he was saying to her. “Liberty . . . and love.”

So wild a dream.